SHE

Alexander Bentley is a gentle soul and a weaver of deep words. Words that carry the weight of even deeper meanings. From his hand drips the softest of whispers. His caress is poetry. His muse, the moon, reflecting light into every fiber.

Nothing is as enchanting as crossing paths with poetry that is filled to the brim with love. The heart speaks a hundred tongues and they are all found inside a single breath. In a single book like this.

The reader is immediately pulled from their chair. Gravity no longer exists here. The soul is drawn in by the tides that flow gently into wanting palms.

While reading, my heart whispered to me. It told me that *She* is the result of what any soul hopes to be to another. It wants to be held. As a reader, I feel embraced. And I can't help but smile.

Alexander, who I deeply admire, invites you in. To make a temporary home. To smile, to play, to feel the heat of passion, to celebrate unconditional love. And for hopeless romantics like myself, you will dare to believe in love again.

An acquired taste for any soul that wishes to embrace the boundless love that fills these pages.

- S.A. QUINOX, AUTHOR OF IMMORTALIS

From *New York Times* Bestselling Author

From a poet to a poet, your writing
is good. If you keep writing you
can get your works published.

Much love,
Atticus

The Ship of the Starved (short story)

Eversleep: The Beauty of Dark Silence

The Raven Redux & Other Poems

Black Mirror: A Book of Sayings

A Poet's Manifesto

SHE

ALEXANDER BENTLEY

A LOVE STORY TOLD IN VERSE

For Jesa

CONTENTS

I've known Alexander Bentley for many years and through those years, I've come to admire his body of work. All of it. The books, the poems, and the quotes he posts on social media almost every day. The one thing that gets me about his poetry, even in a few short lines or a single verse, is that he always draws me into a scene.

Of course, my heart leapt out of my chest the very moment Alexander asked me to read an advanced copy of his newest book, *She*. Without a second thought, I jumped at the chance to be one of the first to read it.

An entire book of poems, a novel based on his own personal love life, a poetic novel if you will. A book that draws the reader in, scene by scene, into the chase, courtship, and tragedies of Night and Luna. The story's two characters —the poet and the muse.

As I read the story, it made me wonder, has Alexander been secretly planning this book all along. For anyone who has been following him for the last year, you'd think he just randomly posted poems on social media. But now, I see there has always been a genius to his madness. And with this book, he's pulled all of those beautiful, relatable and heart touching poems together into a fast-paced, cohesive page-turning story —a masterpiece of literature.

For any of his longtime fans—like me—there are some alternative versions of his popular poems, as well as previously unpublished ones too. But no matter what version of a poem that appears in this collection, the most important thing is that you get to read a gripping story about the struggle of love, set amid the real life pandemic that altered all of our lives.

Before you dive nose deep into the book, there's one last thing that I want to share with you. Something that I'm almost too embarrassed to tell.

When Alexander wrote his darker poetry, I constantly kept thinking this guy must be Edgar Allan Poe reincarnated. His older poems and books, before *She*, often covered subjects of death, depression, and emotional turmoil, and his words in some unknown way would grip onto you and seep into your soul. Just like Poe's poems and stories do.

After reading *She* multiple times and seeing how the author has reinvented himself, I'm now beginning to think Alexander Bentley is a modern-day Shakespeare.

But I'll let you be the judge of that!

- ATLEY, POET

The year was 2019, before the world knew anything about coronavirus, lockdowns and a global pandemic. When things were safe. Much safer.

It was autumn in America, the month of red leaves, pumpkins and Thanksgiving, when fate's brush strokes caused my muse to crash into me. And just like that, in one fell swoop, she swept me up into a sudden storm of passion. A typhoon of emotions I dare not escape and carted me off to her land of enchantment.

Her name: Jesa Cordero. A young beautiful Filipina, born and raised in the Philippines—the home of 7,000 islands.

She's charming, funny and incredibly photogenic. And although she claims she isn't sweet, I often see it. Because she's sweet to her family, her friends, and to the people who matter to her most.

Besides her tender heart, there was something else below the surface. Something inside her soul that spoke to me. Outside observers might call it chemistry or attraction, or perhaps label it destiny or magic.

But whatever it was, it was real.

As a poet falling in love, I naturally wrote Jesa heartfelt

poems and love letters. Words that expressed my attraction and admiration of her beauty. Words that described my love and longing for her. And to this very day, I continue to write her sweet missives.

The woman featured in the book cover's artwork is Jesa. She is Luna. And Luna is *She*. The central character you'll be reading about in the pages that follow. The prize of my eye.

This book is a love story told in poetic verse. A romantic gesture to my Luna. One long love letter chronicling the romance and the chase—how the Night, against all odds, tried to capture the Moon.

But how did Jesa become Luna—the brightest body in the Night's sky?

Even before we started dating, we gave each other cute nicknames. Nicknames that best reflected the qualities we first noticed in each other. And I weaved those into a poem —a double couplet.

Then I posted it on social media, in the most public and transparent place of them all. And the world read the poem, and they loved it.

Since that time, millions of people the world over have read the brief, four-line poem.

During the height of the pandemic, when the world was scared of what was to come and faced orders to stay at home, over 10 million people read it. Becoming what I believe to be the most popular poem of 2020—the Pandemic Year.

Over time, that poem developed into something beyond my control. My most dedicated fans were eager to hear more about the Night and Luna saga.

So this book is really a novel. And it tells the true life story of Night and Luna. Through a collection of poems.

A tale of romance, love and longing. A story of self-discovery and self-reflection. Of dreaming dreams of a future. Of overcoming distance. And overcoming obstacles.

I believe if the English Romantic poet, John Keats, had lived longer, he would have penned a book or dozens of books to his muse, Fanny Brawne. I imagine the great poet would've written, published and dedicated those masterpieces to the affections of her heart and their timeless love.

So in that vein, I invite you—my dear reader—to step into the world of a poet and his muse. To experience the raw emotion of a poet's heart pouring out onto the page.

It's time to take a journey with Night and Luna.

Alexander Bentley
Alajuela, Costa Rica
Tuesday, July 6, 2021

She called me Night,
Because I loved the darkness

And I nicknamed her Luna,
Because she reflected the sun

NIGHT

LUNA

Bright star! would I were steadfast as thou art—
Not in lone splendour hung aloft the night

- JOHN KEATS

There was madness
In between the chaos
Of a dream—in between
Where I was alone
Waiting for a feeling
To sweep me away

And that is when
I found her in the moon
On a dark and sleepless night

And there I was, looking up
Stargazing—pulled in

Consumed by the currents
Of her magnetic beauty

That night, as I walked the streets
I got drunk on the stars
How they glimmered
Across her eyes

Merry-go-round
I was spinning
But for a moment, the world stood still
And all I saw was her beauty
All I saw was her light

She pierced my soul
With a look. And I—
I was hers

The glint in her eyes
Was filled with playfulness
And it reminded me
Of the moon, mysterious
Glistening off the lake
Where I could see
Like a pleasant dream
My reflection too

I never set out to be a selenophile
But somehow I was

Like field mice
Who hope to find their harvest
In cast down moonbeams

Long before I knew your name—
Before it took shape on my lips—
I felt a fluttering in my heart
And I knew, then, it was you

I write about love because I can
Because I know the aching of your heart
That you want to be loved
And to love deeply. Secretly
Yearning for the one. And
With this poem, I hope you
Meet me in the middle, so we can start.

I thought I could save myself
From the rhythm, from the blues
And everything that bleeds

But I was wrong
Your love is the one thing
This beating heart needs

I write myself into dreams
Between whispers
And between the trees
Everywhere you are
And every place you go

Invisible kisses so soft
On the nape of your neck

When I think of poetry
I think of you, I think of us

I watch you from across the room
Sitting cross-legged on the sofa

You light a cigarette and bring it
To your mouth, to your lips
Parted ever so slightly

Enticing me as you exhale clouds
Of pure white smoke

Cherry hot and rosy cheeks.

And without you knowing it
You've seduced me

Stoking the flames of my desire
Just one more slow drag to set me free.

She's so beautiful
When I look at her
I forget to breathe

My muse
My inspiration

A beacon of light

Absorbed in
Thoughts of her

She shines
And everything
Feels just right

I want to live inside her poetry
Nestled between the verses
Strewn between the lines
Sway to the beat of her meter
Dance with her in the moonlight
All to feel her wild little universe

The moon is a lover, too
A trembling shadow in the sky
Weaving its way up to our souls
Then, like that, we're pulled
From the deepest slumber

Maybe, I was born

To be single, destined
To be alone, to find
Comfort in the dark

After all, our dying
Breath is our own

If love were a potion
It'd come sealed in a glass bottle.

We could admire it
The beautiful mesmerizing liquid

Swishing back and forth
As we moved it from side to side.

Or we could be one of the rare few
That didn't let it sit

On the shelf, and drink
From its sweet succulent nectar.

I would choose the latter.
And I would choose to drink it with you.

My entire life
I felt homesick
A stranger
With no place
To lay my head.

When I met you
I realized, that whole time
I was really just
Missing you.

Do you see
Those stars
Up in the sky?

I'd pull them down
If it meant a lifetime
Of happiness with you

Don't falter, don't shake
Fall into the moment
Because you know
You deserve this—
A little bit of happiness

I know the exact moment it happened
You were laughing only the way you do
And then you shot me the warmest smile
Right then, I knew, I was in love with you

A man in love is a man
On the brink of madness
There is genius in his chaos
And chaos in his confidence
And a swelling of the heart
That grips onto everything
He is about to become

If you find me—
Let it be somewhere
Between now and forever

Walking through galaxies
Along the shores of time

Or under lush green trees
On black sandy beaches
Where dreams come true

Not even the gods, in all their glory
With their pandemonium and pandemic
Could ever keep me from loving her

It was long before
I'd hold your hand in mine

And the truth is I had no idea
I'd fall in love with you

But I did. And it was from
The very first moment

Before I could even blink
My eyes.

I find you often in my dreams
Amongst the pines, or on the beach
Or maybe standing on a balcony
Where your silhouette is framed
By the backdrop of the water
And you close your eyes to dream
You're dreaming, dreaming of us

For you—

I have been saving myself
All my life, waiting on you
In quiet solitude, pretending
The wait didn't weigh me down
Hoping you'd come sooner than later

But I realized
You can't rush destiny
And now I know you came—
At the perfect moment, quietly
In the most perfect way
Because you're mine

Like a beautiful sunflower
Found on the unbeaten path
Far from the city limits.

And you bloom, only for me

From this point forward
Everything will change

Because I am set on a path
One of destiny, a quest
For discovery, and there is
No turning back

Taste it once
And the spell of its enchantment
Will never let you be

- LANGSTON HUGHES

And like magic
She left a little bit
Of her soul
Everywhere
She went

Some people say the sky is her second home.
It's because she loves to dream.

And when she looks up at the stars
They shimmer and fill her world with magic.

There—her imagination is free to roam.

You hold a map
Of the stars within
Your pregnant palms
And I hope one day
You'll guide me home

Because these nights—
These lonely nights—
Are all too dark
And suffocating

She is my moon
The queen of the night

And I am darkness
The chaser of her light

"I love looking at the moon," he said.

"Me too," she said.

"It reminds me of you."

"How so?"

"Because you light up the night."

"Then hold my hand," she said.
"And let's watch it glow."

For many a year—
Sorrow was a friend of mine
We spun frantically in the night;
But now, I dance with another—
I dance along to her rhythm
In the blushing moonlight

Most nights
I cannot tell
The difference
Reality
Or a dream

Am I sleeping
Am I awake

It is those fingers
Her touch, the warmth
Of her soft skin that I feel

When she is in my dreams
On those dark nights, it is always real

It's magical, this feeling
The way she makes me feel
I'm falling in love. No, I'm in love
I'm floating on clouds, and she holds me
In her sweet embrace. I'm spellbound
In this holy place, held
Captive, held
In her love

Falling in love
Is shattering a world
Made of glass

The pieces fall
All around your feet
And you don't care

She's a moon beam

But—

She's the kind of light
Only the strongest
Hands
Can hold

I was never a traveler
But through her eyes, I started to see
The world for the very first time

Meet me in the perpetual space
Between your dreams
Between the impossible and possible
Where ideas are born, and I swear
By the last breath in my lungs
I'll show you a lifetime
Of love

Rip me at the seams
And pull me apart

But put me back together
And replace this darkness
With the light of your love

The sound that seeps in
Haunts me like your ghost

Arriving like a thrum
Through the thick walls

Of silence and of pain
A tiny bird's heart beating

Lost in the angry rain

When the moon hangs low
I hear you calling me
Pulling me closer to
The place I want to go

Draw me to your river
Let me wade in the deep
And drink from your waters

Push me under the current
Pin me down
Let me drown
Drown, drown

Drown forever in your love
Hold me here while I am weak

Meet me in the rain
Below the cover of dark clouds
Where the moonless night meets our love
And let's watch the sky fall down
Behind closed eyes
In a downpour of kisses

I'd wait a lifetime for you
Or a thousand
Because I'm pulled
To you like gravity

I will search for you
Your mass, your touch
A way to feel
Your skin on my skin
Just to see
Your bare naked soul again

Teach me about love, about magic
Tell me the secret to casting spells
And how you hold up the universe
So gently in the palm of your hands

These mad lies we tell ourselves
Mind tricks we sell ourselves
All to convince ourselves

That this attraction is
Anything but physical
And that somewhere
In this magical universe
Love might truly exist

It's where I chase you freely
On cloud tops and starry whispers
But I wouldn't have it any other way
And not with anybody else

Because my paper soul yearns
To drink from the galaxies hiding
In your heart, and to soak up
Every ounce, and every last drop
Of who you are

What is our love story
But a tale of two hearts
Coming together as one?

Longing for each other
In the dark of night
Creating flames of passion

I'd split the world in two
Just to have you for a day
Now imagine what I'd do
For a lifetime

If destiny comes to help you
Love will come to meet you

- JALAL AL-DIN RUMI

It takes you by surprise when
That one lover, through an act
Of serendipity, enters your life

Time slows down between
The flutters of your heart
And the blinks of their eyes

Your world, your life, your breath
Falls into the softness of their light

And there is a single moment—
A revelation, when you know
Everything you wanted

Is no longer just a dream

I found myself when I met you
And in that moment
My loneliness was gone

My dearest moon
How you call out for me
In the bellows of the night

Growing in size, growing—
Growing with delight

There is magic
In my poetry
How I fill
Pages of paper
With my love

Our love story is only beginning
And we are on the edge of a promise
Of a future of our own making

It starts again
With a look
With a kiss

Morning, afternoon or night
No matter what time of day
You are my favorite part.

After their midnight rendezvous,
the Poet went home and wrote
Luna a short poem:

We are all fragments
Lost souls, dreaming ourselves
Into existence
One night at a time

And you, my love
Are my beautiful dream

He said . . .

"I know you long for something more
Something much deeper
Something you've never had before."

He said . . .

"I'm right here, standing at your door
Ready to love
You"

He said . . .

"Give me your hand, let's go
For a walk. Go on
A journey. And explore a future
Inevitable."

She said . . .

"This is the kind of love
I need
A love that doesn't hide
Behind the pain."

She said . . .

"So don't be afraid. Show me your face,
The scars, the shadows."

She said . . .

"I want it all. Every part.
The fragile little things
You hide in the dark."

She said . . .

"Give me your love. And this I promise you,
I'll be your moon."

"All I have ever wanted
Is to love
And to be loved," he said.

"Then let me love you," she said.
"Like the moon loves the night."

And the Poet continued
to write and pen her poems:

Eventually, everything collides
So it was only a matter of time
That our two hearts would connect.
Whether it was in the stardust of space
Or under the fading light of paradise

He told her . . .

"In my eyes, nothing is more beautiful
Than the light of your presence."

"A million suns could never compare
With your radiant beauty
Dancing in the sky."

And she just looked at him
With a glint in her eyes
And smiled like a thousand sunflowers
Greeting the day

Why settle for less
Than extraordinary

When you were born
With stars in your eyes

And the universe bursting
Out from your soul?

She told him, "A soulmate is a mirror."

"How is that?" he asked.

"Because, when I look at you,
I don't just see you. I see myself.
A beam of light, reflecting back to me."

Who am I beyond the bridge
Beyond those moments without you
Without you in my arms

I am nothing, without your touch
Without the glint in your eye
Shining back at me

Like a mirror, reflecting
The best parts of my soul

Two planets
Satellites
In motion
Orbiting
Our own paths
But we were always
Destined
To collide

When you feel it
In the fluttering of your heart
Before it blooms a thousand roses
With as many petals as sun rays
Bright and warm like the first spring day

I stand before you naked
Baring my body, baring my soul
Do you see me for who I am?
Do you see the whole?

At dawn, I watch her smile
And flirt with the sky

Taking in the last
Of the fading
Crescent moon

Watching it
Disappear into
The blur of the big blue

And I know she knows
That this love is true

As true and as big
As the great expanse
Above

Your skin, a map
Tracing fingers
Where I want to go
Destinations and constellations
Places I want to know

What is that I hear when you sleep?
The rising and falling breath
The beating heart inside your chest
The life of the one who loves me
Tenderly, sweetly, softly

She was blooming
Like a sunflower
Full of smiles

Blushing, heart deep
And rooted in love

Every time she sees flowers
At the market
Her eyes light up
And it reminds me
Of the first time
I bought her a bouquet
Of sunflowers and tulips
For our first Valentine's Day

I want to be a different kind of ghost
Not the type that leaves your texts
On seen or read

Or the type that never talks to you again
I want to be an apparition, white
On the black of night

The haunting kind, that lives
Inside your head

Where you can't stop yourself from
Thinking about me

And all the beautiful things we will be

I'm in a love affair with poetry
And I love the way she moves
Possessing me like a ghost
One that never quite goes away
And I sway with her between
The lines, in perfect rhythm
Dancing on the motion of her
Syllables, the flick of her tongue

In your silence, I find love
In your eyes, I find magic

In the orange and yellow
Hues of the sun, I find your heart

Burning
Burning for me

I speak a language only she hears
And although the moon rises
And remains silent
She listens, in the pale swell
Of nature's delight, and we're together
In this moment—perfectly planned

We are the naked ones
A halo of kisses
Shrouded in mystery
Wrapped around our heads

Moonlight, moonshine
Electricity in the air
Electricity everywhere
Tangled under the sheets

Melodies between our skin
Enticed by our foreplay
Intoxicated by your touch
Not sure what comes next

Caressing my soft hair
On the edge of pleasure
Seduced by atomic passion
Touch me, tease me
And I am yours

Right here, now
In this foreign land
Cradled by the moon
And your warm embrace

Each time you touch me
I break into particles—
Millions of tiny universes

Like billions of galaxies
Swirling behind my chest
Where time stops to rest

And now, I believe—
I believe in science
The science of us

A love so deep
It overwhelms me
Like an ancient tide

Smear your lipstick
Across my neck

Sweet nectar
From your lips

Until I can't taste anything
But

Your honey

If Sunday never comes
At least I will have tasted
Your honeysuckle lips

We go out into the desert
So we can hold the sun

We escape the heat
Under the cover of a tree

We stand watching
The rays of the gods

And we taste the colors
Yellow and pink
Orange and you

And then
We ached
In awe

At the moment

At how it
Swept us
Away

Into the pines

Like we
Were born
As trees

She came to me
She came to me silently
In the cover of the darkness
When the willows were weeping
And tears stained the pores of my face
She held my hand and wiped away the fear
Now—here we stand, in the moonlight
Waiting for our tomorrow to come

You make me rise before the sun
You make me do terrible, wonderful things
Like hiding under these sheets in the night
Just to feel heaven on the tips of my fingers
As I watch you squirm under my touch
I watch you bite your lips in ecstasy
And nothing compares to this

The soul of the sun
Is in your hands

The blood of my heart
Is in your veins

When you breathe
I breathe

And we are one

Hold me like the sun holds the day
With arms as long and as strong as rays
Let me feel the fire of your embrace

I soaked in the light of your sun
Just to feel your warm embrace

I glided on the stars of the night
To touch the sparkle in your light

And I dipped in your cool oceans
To know the depths of your heart

And what I found along the way
Was beauty in your play

Those birds chirping
They sing for you
They sing for me
They sing for us

And love isn't a curse
But a melody
And I hear it sung
From the trees

I wrapped myself
In the fragrance
Of her perfume

In the silk of her skin
Under bed sheets
Wanting more

And now I am left
With her scent
Mixed with sweat

Her body carved
Into my palms

The wind whispered its name
Said to the distant bird
"This is where I go at night"
But she was not a bird
She was an angel in flight

I don't just love her for the way
She makes me feel. But also
The way she playfully dances
With my demons—
Jealously, fear and insecurity—
And how at the end of each day
She calms the wild torrents within

She tells me, *Love love ko ikaw*
And I say back, *Love love ko din ikaw*

It's true, I love her too

In fact, I'm the one who said it first
Because secretly I always knew
I would marry her

There is nothing but the sun in her eyes
A blue jay sings when she opens her mouth
When she kisses me, there's a gentle breeze
Upon my skin, and I know this is what
Heaven, in all its glory, must be like

I find hope in your touch
Like the last sliver of sunset
And just like that, I know
Everything will be alright

I am enamored with her soul
And I have never felt as alive
As I do when she is loving me

I've waited a lifetime for you
Decade after decade
Down, depressed

But look at us, happily together
And I can finally say,
"Love at last."

Be near me now
My tormenter, my love, be near me—
At this hour when night comes down

- FAIZ AHMED FAIZ

And just like that
We were done
She was gone

No apology
No remorse
No sound

Silence
In rooms
Of emptiness

A dog yelping
Outside, wanting
Back indoors

Where
The heart
Is warm

I read the poetry in your scars
The pelting pain of your past
And with everything you've been through—
Don't you know—
Doesn't make you any less
Beautiful

What if I told you
That you were enough
That all the hardships
All the cruel people
Everything bad
Has led to this

To see, feel and
Breathe a love like this

So take it all in
Breathe in deep
And never let me go

A woman in love
Is a woman blooming
Like a sunflower
Delicate and sweet
She opens for the sun
And stays open
Through the storms
The wildest of rains

She felt there was no magic in her stars
No one noticed her beauty
Even when she shined in all her glory

But before daybreak, her sadness faded away
Because she knew the Night loved her

Even in the torrent of moods
I still love her. How could I not?

There are fires on the plains
And rivers in her valley
There is light and there is water
There is heat and there is life

Don't be afraid to feel
To fight for a fairytale
Those perfect moments

Where love is real
And love is anything
But magic

And if I could catch
But one of her teardrops
On the end of my fingertip
Then I'd know the weight
Of her pain

To love a poet
Is like having the universe
Pour itself into your soul
With all its madness

To die as wild Romantics
Is to die with the holy breath
Of the universe in our lungs

Little by little, like a skillful technician
You have mysteriously opened me up.
But soon, you will crack me wide open.
And let out my light.

Let your labor be a masterpiece. A spectacle.
A vista of love that shines on and on. And we
Can shine together for the rest of our lives.

In motion. Like waves. Dancing in the dark.
Cutting spaces. Lost at the edge.

And my love, my sweet sweet love, we shall
Make it beautiful and bright.

To love is also to forgive
Because no matter how much
Two longing souls are attracted
No relationship is perfect

And all that I can say for today
Is that I am sorry for all the ways
I have caused you pain

Even the pain to come
But there is no amount of rain
That will keep me from staying

I just hope your tears turn to seeds
So I can be here to watch you bloom

Love comes at a price
And only those willing
To speak the currency
Discover its treasure

Into wild hearts we go
On the banks of foreign towns
Where the unknown vulture
Hunts down innocent prey
But I wouldn't have it any other way
Because that is love

I tremble with fear, earthquake emotions
My feet, unstable and unsteady
I fall

I fall into your grace, your love, your presence
And you lift me up
Once again

Bit by tiny bit
I have poured
My broken pieces
Into hands that hold me

From your palms
I have watched
Delicate flowers bloom

Beautiful isn't always perfect
Sometimes there's hidden things
Well below the surface of the skin
Fragile things that'll never been seen
But that doesn't make you any less
Beautiful

The problem with love is that you give
Your whole heart or you don't
And both have their consequences
You float like a dove's feather
Or you fall like gravity

Love without the thrill of romance
Is a villain on a dark and lonely road
A thief in the middle of the night
Stealing our hearts, stealing our light

Our love was made for poetry
To be written, to be read
Let my words seep into your soul
And let them bring you back to life

Love is more than fire in the sky
It is about holding each other
In the dim darkness
When things are at their worst
But as long as I have you
You will always be my bright star
My guiding light
Even on the blackest of nights

My eyes are tethered to her soul
Through a looking glass I see

The stars, the moon, the galaxy

Everything that swirls inside her
She waits—waiting to be freed

He stole flowers—
From broken pots—
To watch them grow

And he planted—
A secret garden—
In her fragile heart

Where sunflowers—
Found the daylight—
Amongst a fresh start

I can't sleep tonight
Without hearing your voice one last time

But there's echoes on the other end of the line
And the weight of the phone is sinking
Into my sweaty hand

Heavy from all the wrong things that I said

You have been
Mending my heart
Slowly. Meticulously
With patience. Creating
A new masterpiece
From the broken pieces

I know what I lost

A woman so remarkable
That the gods themselves
Would worship at her feet
If they knew her secret
Hiding place on earth

But I'm not done fighting
For what I believe in

Because there is no distance
That will keep me from you

Not the ends of the earth
Nor the highest mountains
Nor sailing the seven seas
Will keep me from holding
You in my arms once more

I found a way out of the darkness
And it was through the light in your eyes

In this mad hour
When all is strange
And I am bursting with love
No one can tell me how to live

I have a heart
Darkened by the past
But I still cling to love

I cling to you

Like you're my last breath

We made it through the night, you and I
And we survived it all, we survived the fall
The rain, the storm, the violent bucking sea

It's morning, we're resting under the tree
You look so peaceful with two closed eyes
And I'm just grateful you made it out alive

I found a way out of the pain
Through the cracks in your heart
And that's where you showed me
You showed me the light

I know I get angry sometimes
But somehow you quiet the storm

It must be your tender spirit
How you stay calm in the wild rain

And even if I might be a howling wind
You stare at me and I slow down

Until the raging weather within
Comes to an end

Hold my hand
Tell me how much
I still matter

And I'll do the same

Because I never
Want to stop holding
Or telling you

I got you through it all

Even if it means we
Have to walk through
The fires

If life has taught me
There are good days
There are bad days too

And I want them all with you
Cuddled together on the lake
Taking in the last of the moon

Find a love
That holds you
Even while
The world
Sleeps

When I look into her eyes, I see infinity

I glimpse the stars, the moon
And the planets swirling

And I'd travel there and back just to be
With her again

Hope is the thing with feathers
That perches in the soul
And sings the tune without the words
And never stops at all

- EMILY DICKINSON

Hold her like tomorrow may never come
Like there's a true risk you could lose her
Tonight. And if you did, nothing
In this world
Would ever be the same

The edge of tomorrow
May never exist
Let's go out back
Sit on the porch
Cast our eyes on the fading sun
Watch it burn!
Oh, let's watch it burn!

She is my safe place
Artwork on the fringe
Everything I wanted
And everything I need

I will love you with every breath
Every laugh, every sigh, and every kiss

Through all the chaos
In each waking moment
And in every dream. I will love you
Even after my brittle bones
Grind to dust

I hold your name on my breath
Like the last sip of cold beer
On a hot summer day

And I'm drunk on your love
Reeling in this moment
Feeling the pulse of our play

And here again, I'm lost within your eyes
Giving you every reason to stay—

And you stay
On the cusp of this dream forever

With me

Keep me
Like the rivers keep the rain
Like the earth collects the dust
Like the night holds the moon

Stay here in this moment forever
Where everything we are is now
And everything is brand-new

Together their bodies were like poetry
Two verses stacked one on top of the other
Only a tiny space separating them
That is until they became
One verse, flowing wild and free

You're my one and everything
My world, my galaxy, my universe

And I'm amazed at your beauty
All the stars shine for you
Casting their light, a glow, on your face

There's a death rattle
Shaking in my bones
Shaking like a thunderbolt
And with my time left on earth
I don't care where we go
As long as I'm with you
And we call it home

She touched angels with her lips
And made me realize that Death
Is but only a temporary vacation

Through all the phases of the moon
When summer passes and winter is home
On cold nights that turn to blue
I know now that I will still be loving you

I want to give you all of my love
Every day, every ounce, every drop

Until this heart is tired and spent
Exhausted from all the giving

And only then will I be the most
Beautiful version of who I can be

I wake up on a Tuesday morning
In a hotel room with a loft

We're naked in a queen bed
Half covered by the sheets

I'm exhausted, you're spent
But I'm half-awake

Our skin is touching
Your black hair is a mess

And last night—last night
You felt like heaven

I kiss your pillow at night
In the shadows of still moonlight

For every day we are apart
I pray to keep you in my heart

Paying soft tributes with my lips
Until the moment I hold your hips
And finally, at last, look into your eyes

On restless nights like this
When half the world is asleep
I look at the moon and think

Thinking of a future with you
Dreaming until the sky is blue
Dreaming with eyes open

Hearing your name softly spoken
And that's when I feel your lips
I feel your touch, I feel your kiss

I cannot promise this body shall stay forever
But I can say, I shall love you now and always

Even when I am gone, my love will remain
And one day we will meet again

All my life

I found little
Pieces of her

Scattered
Across time

In places
I would go

Guiding me
Back home

I built a home
Among the stars
And wrote your name

So look up
To the sky
And meet me there

It's a thing of beauty
How I think deeply about the future
For I know, it holds the ocean in your eyes

From the beginning til the end of time
Her heart was, is and has been mine
In dark skies, her light
Like the moon belongs to the night

I love her. All this time I have loved her
From the very beginning until now

And the embers still glow hot, as I sacrifice
My heart on the coals of this great white heat

And it's all for her

I touch forever
Every time I look
Into your eyes

Tomorrow is a myth
Like nocturnal wonders
That never come true
But I'd wait forever
If it was for you

If I played the part of God
Even for the briefest of hours
I would have done the same

I would have arranged the stars
And the world for us to meet
Moving people and parties into action
Just so our wayward paths would cross

And after all I have seen of us, I know
There are no accidents—this is our fate

If our days must be numbered
By the hands of God
Then I'll love you so madly
It stops the revolutions of the sun
And the only ones left spinning
Will be us

If I were to one day
Reincarnate and come back
To a new lifetime
I would wish for it to be as a tree
And you as a butterfly
So you could hug me
And kiss me with the gentle fluttering
Of your wings
That way you could fly and then be free

Dream with me a thousand nights
Under skies of rain and clouds of lies
Dream with me a thousand lies
Until we banish the emerald light
Dream with me a thousand times
As we live the plays we write

You cannot conceive how I ache to be with you:
how I would die for one hour

- JOHN KEATS

Her beauty haunts me
In the peripheral
With my eyes shut

I still see the features
Her delicate face
Lingering on the edge
Of the darkness

Brighter than the silhouette
Against the moon
Caramel skin
Golden undertones

Dimples when she smiles
At me
And those luscious lips
That invite me in

A beautiful dark mole above
Her mouth
Waves of her long hair hanging down
And those big bold eyes
Staring into my soul

It's not only the beauty of her
It's really the bleeding elegance of her
Soul and if I could
Take my childhood camera and snap
Her essence I would keep
That Polaroid forever
Safely tucked away
In my book of memories

With this global pandemic
Some days are a battle
And some nights are a war
But through it all
I know truth

You can't quarantine love
Because it's too contagious
And it will always run free

Through the parks, in the streets
And at home, for those keeping score

I will hold onto you through these tough
And turbulent times, when the world is bleak
And uninviting. When hope seems to be a
Distant memory. And I will invite you in
To stay, to make a home, to play.
To celebrate our love.

For our love is stronger than this. It will last
A thousand lifetimes. Through ups and
Downs, through panic and hysteria.
Through joy and pain. Through life
And death.

For our love is strong—it is stronger
Than this.

In these trying times, I'll find my way to you
Because as far as I see it, your heart
Is my home. The place I belong.
The place I long to be.

So let your soul compass guide me back
Through the chaos, through uncertainty
And as surely as I love you with every fiber
And every pound of flesh, I'll find you again

Love is not tourism
Or a crime
So why treat
Long distance lovers
Like caged animals?
Locked up and apart
Forced to spend
The holidays alone

Who will finally let
Them be together?
Like the stars
Destined them to be

Don't you see
That it's time you steal?

The planes aren't flying
The ports are closing
Travel is restricted

But I'm fighting my way to you
Every day

And I'd do anything to get there

I'll stow away on a cargo ship
Ride the great Pacific Ocean
For months on end
If it means I get to see you
Standing face to face

At the edge of our future
True love knows no distance
No boundaries, no consequence

For when two hearts are entwined
They are so meshed together
Not even the gods can break them apart

Love is a voice in the sea
Lost on the waves, whispering
Your name. Whispering—

"Come home, come home."

I may have learned a thousand things
A hundred thousand. But after all
I have learned, I only know one truth
That my love, for you, will never die

I'd die for you
Like Romeo
For his Juliet
In a twist of fate
As long as it meant
We'd be together, forever
In the afterlife

Soulmates, entwined
Like fine crafted glass
On a lake of fire, bring me to the edge
Lay me down, hold my hand
Make me forget, see you
In the next life, see you
On the other side

The sound of your voice
Like soft echoes in the night
The glimmer of your beauty
In the pale sunlight

The palm of your hand
Your touch, on my face
The mysteries
Of your movement
Your grace

All the things I loved
And everything
That never was

The chasm widens
As the weeks and months go by
I fill it with every type of emotion
That I've felt under the sun
And let us not forget
The feelings that come at night
When the moon is at its peak
Hanging and haunting—it's haunting me
Like the pale white apparition, I've become
That's when I lose my mind
In the spirit of madness
Torn between love and tragedy
I plunge into the dark unknown
Without her, losing myself

I need you like the trees need the sun
I need you like the wave needs the ocean
I need you like the birds need the sky
I need you, because you helped me
Spread my wings and learn to fly

There is no distance
No invisible boundary
No amount of time
No line in the sand
No—nothing at all
That can keep me
From loving you

I got you
Like the day has the sun
And the night has the moon

I got you
When your pain is real
And the worst is yet to come

I got you
Now and always
In tears and blood
Distance and forever

I am a lonely house at the end of a dark road
And my wooden doors ache for your presence
Calling you home, to live within these walls
They need the light of your soul

It's lonely in this big bed without you
Wishing the miles between us weren't true

I wake up from a bad dream, my hair
A tangled mess, and you're not here

Your side—the left—is kept
Untouched

And what I need more than ever
Is the sound of your breath
Breathing gently in my ear

I am so crazy in love

I would tear down
The stars from heaven

Rip them right off
Their hinges in the sky

Just to feel your touch

On nights like these—
With a pregnant moon
A blanket full of stars
And a cool breeze
When we're staring up
At the same dark sky
I really can't believe
You're all mine

Tonight, my heart aches for you
While you sleep, while you dream
And I hope, tonight
I'm in your dreams too

I have never counted the days
As diligently as I have these past few weeks

Marking out the calendar
Anticipating the moment
I finally get to see you

I'll sleep well tonight
Knowing you love me too

You cast a fire's glow as our guiding light
To keep us warm from cold, to give us hope
While we travel the uncertain road ahead

And that's why this burning lantern
Shall carry the flame of your heart
Into the darkest shadows of night

Forever
Into the darkness
Until we reach the daylight

The sky is falling
Like melted chocolate
Over my withered bones

And all I want
Is to get back home

To your heart
To the place that
Holds my soul

When that will be
Only heaven knows

I'm counting down the days
Until I hold you in my arms
Like the first time

I spoke softly to her
As if our souls knew no distance
Like she was made for me
And I—made for her

I just can't say I miss you
Because I've missed you every single minute
Of every single hour, of all the days
That you've been gone

I think about you constantly
In the tiny gaps of time
That stand still as ice
On the edge of a sword
And I've never missed anyone
As much as I've missed you

I just can't say the words I miss you
Because it's more than that
But it's just like that
As simple and as complex
Of a truth as it ever will be

So, I'll just say it
Because it's true
I miss you

I've gone mad
Watching the clock
In the moments
Missing you

And after all this time
I can't tell you how
Many hours or days
Have passed since
I last saw your face

When I hear your voice, I feel more.
More human. More alive.
And a lot more love.

Sometimes we would sit in silence
Just staring at each other on video

Face to face, without saying a word
I'd count the rise and fall of her chest

Those breathless moments of beauty
So perfectly spun together

And although we were worlds apart
We felt so close, I'd call her home

I don't want to be haunted by her memories.
But by her presence. By her love. By the way
She touches my arm and runs her fingers
Through my hair. By the way she kisses
My lips and leaves me wanting more.

I dream, I dream of this . . .

To dip my toes in the waters of forever
Slip into the universe of your soul
And never leave our slice of paradise

I find myself on the river
Waiting for you, waiting to talk
About the universe and the stars
How light bends around the earth
Just to get a glimpse of you

And these shadows haunt me
With the sight of your face
Holding onto the memory
The moon could never escape
The orbit of our spinning lake
How you could never quite get away
From me or this place or these times

And surely, one day, you'll return

On a bus she rides with a belly full
Of excitement, she's chasing dreams

One kilometer closer, she's almost there

Almost to the place she belongs

I wish, I wish upon a star
I wish you wouldn't be so far

And tonight the distance
Is pulling me far below

I am caught in the undertow

I touched you last night
In my dreams
The fabric of reality ripped in two
And for a split second, I reached through
Feeling the warmth of your delicate skin

This grief
Bound to me

Heavy as
The snow

Under cover
Of the trees

In a different world
In a different time and place
We might've stood a chance

But as we know now
Luck wasn't on our side
Nor were the Fates

In this mortal life
I shall go wherever
The Fates take me
As long as it's to you

Through these threads of fate
We weep and we cry at night

But in the morning, I rise

And I will keep rising
Until I touch your light

I am so tired of shivering at night
Like the haunting of moonlight

And these muscles ache for you
Like the sun without day

Won't you come back soon
Before my withering bones
Forget how to say your name?

I visit the gardens
Where you left your scent
Now, I close my eyes
And can see your hands
How they touched me
How they caressed my skin
Leaving a subtle imprint

The Night longed for the moon—
She was luminous, ever-glowing

But in all her hypnotic beauty
She remained too far out of reach

The pangs of their divine entanglement
Divided them with a bitter distance

Until one day, she disappeared below
The horizon of a beautiful dim twilight

And there he was, alone, left looking—
Would he ever see his sweet Luna again?

Darkness isn't the absence of light
It's the absence of you. And today
Was the darkest day, missing you
Storms overtook the sky.

I get swept away by thoughts of you
Memories yet to happen. When we're walking
Our kids down the street, hand in hand
A family founded on love.

And this is where it starts. With us. With love
And passion. A foray of fierce kisses. In bed
Keeping each other awake. Wide awake—
Until the night is faded.

She descended
From the stars
Many lifetimes ago
Elusive, she escaped me
For way too long
But I've found her now
In this life where dreams
Come true. And I touched her
Just for a moment

With a smile she left stardust on my skin
Like it was glitter smeared from a jar
That feeling she gives me, it will never fade
Not even when, I am, afar

I awoke from a dream last night
And I remember what I spoke to her

It was this, said truthfully:

"Missing you never felt like forever
Because I knew one day you'd return."

I keep telling myself tomorrow
Will be different. That the clouds
Will part and the dark days
Will move past me.

But it's too hard, too dark here.
Knowing I'm alone.
Without you.

I've been lost for weeks
Without you. Breaking glasses
On the kitchen floor
Just to see if I can put
The pieces back together
But my hands are bleeding
With red ink that you cannot see
This agony, this nightmare
Without you, is too much
The picture in my pocket
Is the only thing that gives me hope
Hope I'll see the glimmering
Light of your face again
Before I swoon
In my dying hour

The truth is she is a mystery, unfolding
One puzzle piece at a time. I didn't know
What would happen next, but I opened
Myself up to a world of possibilities
It's the reason I still want to explore
Every inch of her body, every part
Of her mind, and dwell in the spirit
Of her essence—forever

When I say . . .
"I can't imagine a day without you"
It means I want you in my life every second
Of every hour, of every blazing sunny day

It means the clock would stop spinning
In circles, around the point you have become

But I'll show up every day
In every possible way, dirty or clean
Covered in mud or insanity

Because I have . . .
"I love you, I love you, I love you"
Bursting out the seams of my soul

And I could say those words forever, until
The end of time, until we are made whole.

I am already there with you, when you
Don't see me and when you do. When
You miss me and I miss you. When you
Take a breath, when you blink your eyes.
And when the sun rises and the moon
Comes out at night.

Every minute of every day, I am with you.
I am always with you, wherever you go.
Even when thousands of miles separate us
We are together. For my soul knows nothing
But the tenderness of your soul. And you—
My sweet love, live inside my heart, just
As I live inside yours.

When I finally kiss you
Underneath the light
Of a thousand stars

I will be certain
Our love is not
Just a dream

7 / A LOVE STORY FOR ALL THE AGES

The sight of lovers feedeth those in love

– WILLIAM SHAKESPEARE

She is small, but fierce
She is strength on a hard day
She is wild, she's a muse
Tempting the gods of fate
She is everything, everywhere
She is a recipe for love
And she—she is mine

Here I am again
In your arms
Like it's the first time

And I feel
Nothing but bliss

I found you on the footsteps of forever
Waiting for me late in the cold of night

We lay here, two warm bodies, in a bed
I hope the morning never comes

Baby, I'm so in love with you

Stay with me here, tonight
Through dusk, through darkness
Until the breaking of dawn

When the first rays wash over you
Illuminating your face in morning's light

At dusk you hold onto me
Like the last rays of sunlight
As they vanish below the horizon
And you devour them with your eyes

Don't kiss me softly
Kiss me boldly, madly

Like the rains will never stop
And the clouds will never part
And the sun will never shine

Because all we have is this moment
My beautiful moment with you

I watch her pray in bed
On a street with God
Lighting lampposts prayers
And I sit in silent observation—wondering
What are the thoughts in her head
And whether she's praying for me
Praying for us, praying sweet thoughts
Things that will never be said

While she's sound asleep
Late at night, I write
Writing myself into her dreams

In the early morning light
I love the way your face glows

So tell me my lover
My dearest Luna

How do you sparkle
And light up the day?

How does eternity
Whisper from your eyes?

What is your secret
That holds me enchanted
In your lovely skies?

In my dreams last night
I ascended to the heights of heaven
And saw an angel

In the morning
At the break of dawn
I woke up and she was there

Lying next to me in bed
Naked in all her heavenly brilliance

Just like the day falls to night
And the night fades into the day
I'll be right there loving you
Endlessly, on the other side

The lanterns go out while she sleeps
And she is in a peaceful slumber
Deep within the glowing light of our love
Dreaming, she is dreaming of us?
A future, a family, the promise of forever?

Tell me a story
Of how you got here
And I'll tell you why
The stars shine for you

When you see her, the woman
God carved out for your soul
That's when you'll believe in
Fairytales and magic and
10,000 sunsets together

I believe in love, magic, and us.

Find me where the dark days meet the light
And this I promise you, we can have forever
Lost in the beauty of the dreams we will write

To have you in my life
Like a warm blessing
On a cold winter's morning
Sent by the sun
And like the sun
Let our love rise
Until our bodies are spent
And the twinkling stars
Come undone

Your velvet love brings me to my knees
To your church, to worship at night
Paying homage, speaking in tongues
Between the pillars of delight
I beg for a taste, to drink your wine
Bowing my head to the one I praise

I won't stop writing about love. Or about us
Or how the stars light up your eyes
Your love moves me to do remarkable things
Magical things. Like writing a fairytale
From the stardust of your existence

Love me again
Like it's the first time

Like we never held
The whisper in our breaths

Like we never stopped
The beating of our hearts

Love me again
Today, tomorrow, for all time

I will remember the kisses
I will remember the sun
How you looked the day
When we met
Like a dream, surreal
The way you made me feel

My heart beating
And thumping in my chest
I never thought I would find
My way to you
But I did

There is only one thing
I love more than writing
You

To live and love poetically
Is at the heart of humanity

And with her, love is easy

Today I found an old poem
Tucked away inside a book

Between the lines
I read your name
And it called to me
With love

I love you between the rise and fall
When you are fast asleep and wide awake
When the sun calls and the moon is bright

I love you between the stars and planets
In the darkness of night, where shadows live
And ghosts have long been forgotten

I love you now, in this moment—
Beautifully sweet
Between the cool springtime air
And satin sheets

You reveal yourself under the cover of night
My senses are heightened and full of light
Blood is pumping in our veins
There is attraction, there is heat
There is you and there is me

I am pulled in—
Unswayed, and then—
It is there, where I stare
A tantalizing secret, a lovely thing

I whispered love to your soul
Until the very day I met you
Then I kept whispering
Until you fell in love with me
And now, you're whispering it back too

Once upon a star, I wished to love a girl
Like her. Little did I know, she was falling
From heaven. Lightning fast. And she was
About to crash into my life. Like a comet
Sent down to earth. With all her blazing
Wondrous glory.

And it was with love, and through her love
That I survived.

Love is a tiny window
A glimpse at eternity
And together we get
To behold all its glory
Under the faint stars
Of the ephemeral sky

I love loudly through poems
Through the chill in the air
On a cold winter's night
Through spontaneous
Moments of wild ambition.

When I look at her
I don't want to hold back.
I can barely contain myself.
There is something about her
In the way she walks, in the sound
Of her voice when she talks
In the melody when she sings
That penetrates into the deepest
Unknown parts of my soul.
She is the only woman
The only human being
That could pierce me
As deep as she has.

No one else has come as close.
And I'm afraid no one else will.
But honestly, I only want
To let her in, no one else.
She can have my loud
And she can have my love.
All of it, as wildly as
She comes to me.

Every little poem
Is my way of saying
I love you now
I love you tomorrow
I love you forever

Every moment with you is a syllable
In our evolving language of love

With sweet words spoken from soft lips
I glide slowly, tracing my warm mouth
Around the most delicate areas of your skin

And before this night is over
I will have written a book—erotic
Leaving no part of your body untouched

Sometimes a poem is a love letter
Softly spoken to the universe
Made up of the sweetest sounds

So write your beautiful poems
And send them out into the ether
Because you never know who's listening
And who needs them the most

There may have been a thousand
Love stories since the beginning of time

But ours is my favorite one

I want to tell you "I love you"
A thousand times a day
But it still wouldn't be enough
To express the depth and
Breadth of my love for you

It hangs

In the air between us, the heat
Of flirtatious looks
In silence, the hypnotic spell
Of our never-ending play

Love is like a good book
Not one you devour
In a single setting
One-night stand
A book you absorb
Night after night
In quiet company
A book you read
And re-read
Lost between the covers
Turning the pages
Reading the words
Finding new meaning
And new hope

I collect old books, antiqued copies
Of the classics, ones that people have
Long forgotten as they gather dust
On their covers, sitting alone in a box.
And over the years I have developed
A love for the rare, special beauty.
But until today I have never seen
A thing as rare and beautiful as you.

At the edge of the day
Here in the twilight hour
We walk along hand in hand
On the old streets of Bauan

Two story houses on each side
Lush vegetation reaching for the sky
Headlights flicker in and out of view

Let's find a quiet place to stand
A place to be alone on this sleepy road
To marvel at the beauty of the stars
To marvel at our timeless love

In this world of hate, all I want is you
To sacrifice myself on the altar of our love
To feel the softness of your breath on my skin
To dance in the breeze of the midnight hour
To stroke your hair as we curl up by the fire
To melt into the stars of this heavenly bliss

I want to immortalize you
With love letters and poems

So our love is remembered
Forever and a day, for all
Generations to come

Until the very end, when
The last moon in heaven's sky
Eclipses the dying sun

There is you
And there is me
And then there is us
And that is love

Under the trees of souls
Our roots dig deep
Far into the soil
Spread far
Like spider webs
But somehow
Our paths still crossed
And now it feels
As if we are one soul
United—limitless!

She's the entire universe expanding
A perched bird ready to take flight

A phoenix rising
"Go!" I told her
"Go everywhere
Flap your wings and fly!"

Forever
The light
Of my love
Burns for you

In this dim world
No worries
No more fears
No doubts
No more pain
She was finally
In paradise
Held securely
In my arms
Gentle kisses
On the back of her neck
Sweet sensations
And a beautiful love
Peacefully
We swayed
Into a beautiful sleep
Dreaming dreams
Of one another

The brilliance of your eyes
Makes it that much easier
To fall madly in love
With a woman like you

Crazy as the moon, we love
A silhouette of the past

Burning in the sky, we live
With hearts built to last

You're my favorite excuse
For a lazy Sunday morning
It's in the way you rest
Your head on my chest
And you tell me you're listening
To the sounds of the universe
We could hold this moment
Forever if we stayed right here
Tucked beneath the sheets
Half-awake in our own
Enlightenment

I don't know what it means
But the moon sings your name

There are lessons in life
I can't find in books
But I read them in your eyes

A morning
Without saying
"Good morning"
To you
Is empty

This is our moment
Where we get to shine
Like a thousand suns
From the corners
Of cracked smiles
Drowning in the light
Along the rich coast
Of our little paradise

Is this a dream
Where I float adrift
Amongst the isles?

The soft sounds
Of waves crashing
By my sandy feet

Where the wind
Whips my dark hair
In this green paradise

We're holding hands
With both our feet
Buried in the sand

And our love is real

This dream is real

And the day will never end

Fast asleep
In her slumber-time lull

Over and over, in her dreams
She whispers "I love you"

Because her heart is full

She was, all the light, I ever needed
And now, she is, the only light I see

Let's move slowly
Through the pages
Of our lives
You and I
Where our chapters
Take years
And the years
Become decades

And when I find you
On the other side

Standing at the gates
Of a paradise in the sky

I will hold you like
We never lost a minute
Like we never lost our love

I don't know
How many moments
I have with you
But I'll take them all

Color my soul
In all the beauty
Of the world

As I try to capture
The vibrance of this life
In the palm of my hands

Watching the sun
Dance across the sky—
Blue, gold, and you

Like the bright colors
Of spring will never end
And never give way

Green trees swaying
In the breeze of the day
The movement of life

And I love it when
You are dancing too
Wearing my maroon tee

So wash over me—
Like the afternoon rains
But leave me your colors

Now, let's take in the last
Shred of today's twilight
Greeting the black night

And with a gleeful pride
We sit here nestled
Watching stars come to life

Yellow, silver, and white
And shades of blue too
A glowing moonlight

And let's stay right here
Through the tranquil hours
Until the morning sky is—fire

Dawn is upon us
I see it stretching above
The horizon's early light
Like a candle's wick burning
Dripping with love and romance
And all the hidden treasures
Discovered in the dark
A whisper held silent
A kiss good morning
Your silky soft skin
Warm as the sun

I don't care the sacrifice
Make me bleed a thousand suns
As long as it means your light never leaves

How dangerous
We have become

To be loved
And be in love

And because of it
The world is ours

But all we want
Is one another

Here and now
Always forever

Nothing more

My Luna, my star
Down by the sea

Aglow in the dark
Casting your light

Into the shadows
Of my weary night

Under the palm trees
On shores we meet

Give me your hand
Delicate and sweet

You are my love
And so full of life

So please tell me
You'll be my wife

Through sickness
And in death
I will always love you

Like the autumn leaves
That fall from the tree
I will bloom again
In our springtime paradise

And I will find you
On the other side
Where everything is new

My heart holds so much, it cannot
Be weighed, nor measured, for it
Possesses all of your love.

Every ounce, every drop, every memory
You have given to me. And I keep it safe
In the harbor, where we are anchored as one.

To be the happiest man in the world
I need only two things each and every day:

Number 1
To feel your pulse and breath
As you fall asleep in my arms at night

Number 2
To be reminded of our togetherness
As the sun wakes us up in the morning light

Nothing more and nothing less.

Artwork by Daniela Niegos (August 2020).
Depicting Night and Luna dancing under the stars.

Remember this:

Love is real

Just because
You haven't found it yet
Doesn't mean you
Never will

The multitude of voices echoed through the tiny house, the sound not dimming even slightly after I walked out of the kitchen. My mother and my two older sisters, Jade and Lily, remained at their posts, crammed together by the stove, making arroz caldo, a type of porridge. The smell of chicken and boiled eggs filled the air, making my stomach growl as I walked into the living room, dodging my two older brothers, Allen and Gabriel, as they roughhoused.

I smiled at Joshua, my youngest brother, and swept my hand over the top of his black hair, feeling its softness and fluff. Of all my siblings, he was my favorite.

"Breakfast will be ready soon," I told him, placing my hand on his shoulder and looking over his head at more of my cousins pour into the house. They all made a direct line to the kitchen to talk to my mother and sisters, barely sparing me a glance. It always seemed like a full house around here, but I liked seeing my family around.

"I'm hungry," Joshua murmured, leaning his head against

my arm as he watched our brothers wrestle each other to the ground. He laughed softly with a toothy grin, one of his front teeth having recently fallen out.

"I know," I sighed, feeling my own stomach growl as the delicious aromas poured from the kitchen as they cooked the porridge and other dishes for the family to share. We typically did big meals like that. Despite my body very insistently telling me that I was hungry, I just didn't feel like eating right now. I ruffled Joshua's soft hair before walking to my room.

I grabbed my phone off my desk, deciding to pass the time until breakfast by getting on Facebook. There was nothing else to do. Everyone was doing their own thing. I mindlessly walked back into the living room as I checked my notifications, rolling my eyes at a few messages from a few guys trying to chat with me. They asked me to send pictures to them or to video chat with them. I knew that their intentions weren't pure, prompting me to just block them. I didn't need to have my time wasted by them.

I scrolled down a little to see that I had a new friend request from a man named Alex. I narrowed my eyes a little out of curiosity, not recognizing the man. He must've somehow found me on here. I tapped on his profile, zooming into his profile picture to admire the headshot picture of him. He was older, but he looked professional and charming in a way. I tilted my head curiously, my black hair falling against my shoulders as I smiled to myself. I wondered why he was interested in me out of all people. He was probably married.

I couldn't help but snoop a little through his profile information, noting that he was a writer, which was interesting to me. I wouldn't have pegged him as one, figuring that he worked at a popular company at some desk job. However, I liked that he was a writer and wrote poetry. It was different and romantic in a way, coaxing me to mindlessly chew on my bottom lip as I explored his pictures. He seemed to travel a good bit, visiting places all over the United States from New York City to Los Angeles.

"What are you looking at?" Jade's voice sounded behind me suddenly.

I jumped a little at her words, my eyes widening as I spun around, like I had been caught doing something that I wasn't supposed to. I calmed my heart rate, knowing that it really wasn't a big deal. These things never panned out anyway.

ACKNOWLEDGMENTS

My Fans—wherever you are in the world. Thank you for all of your support. Many of you have watched the real life story of Night and Luna unfold. And with your encouragement, you helped me bring this story to life.

Kerry Wade—the book's editor. I am grateful for her work and contribution, in arranging and editing this collection. Otherwise, I would have been lost pulling it all together and telling a cohesive, memorable story.

My Mother—the reason I am alive. I could never describe how much I owe you, for giving me life. For taking me from a battered home and helping me be the man I am today.

And last, but not least . . .

Jesa Cordero—my bebe. This book would have not been possible without you and your love. Unquestionably, you are my bright star—my moon!

Alexander Bentley is a wordsmith, inkslinger, poet.

He started posting his poems online in 2014, first on Tumblr and then shifted to Instagram when he discovered typed quotes from R.M. Drake. Alexander now ranks as one of the top poets on Facebook, alongside Rupi Kaur, Lang Leav, Pierre Alex Jeanty, and the poet who inspired him to post on social media in the first place.

Alexander's body of work touches most commonly on themes of death and loss, depression and heartbreak, life and hope, but most importantly: love.

Since he started dating his Filipina girlfriend Jesa in November 2019, Alexander has been very vocal about their relationship on social media. Which has helped him find new audiences for his poetry while encouraging people from different cultures and all walks of life to embrace the love inside their hearts.

facebook.com/abentleywrites

twitter.com/abentleywrites

instagram.com/a.bntly

goodreads.com/alexander_bentley

Glimpse into the real life Night and Luna saga as it unfolds on social media, where the couple share a behind the scenes look with their fans.

facebook.com/NightandLuna

www.ingramcontent.com/pod-product-compliance
Lightning Source LLC
Chambersburg PA
CBHW021100110726
47900CB00007B/1959